T0156877

Self Infinity

Freedom from the World of Projection

Jennifer D. Ables, PhD
Edited by Emily Schulz, PhD

iUniverse, Inc.
New York   Bloomington

Self Infinity
Freedom from the World of Projection

iUniverse books may be ordered through booksellers or by contacting:

iUniverse
1663 Liberty Drive
Bloomington, IN 47403
www.iuniverse.com
1-800-Authors (1-800-288-4677)

Because of the dynamic nature of the Internet, any Web addresses or links contained in this book may have changed since publication and may no longer be valid.

ISBN: 978-1-4401-9494-8 (sc)
ISBN: 978-1-4401-9495-5 (ebk)

Printed in the United States of America

iUniverse rev. date: 12/1/2009

For those who wish to Awaken and be Free

To family, friends and teachers
Thank you for all the Love, support and guidance,
seen and unseen.

CONTENTS

CHAPTER ONE –
SELF REALIZATION

WHAT IS SELF REALIZATION?

Have you ever wondered what you really are, why you are here, or what God is? Self Realization is a deep and lived understanding of these things. The term can be used to describe the clarity and realization of the answers to some of life's conundrums. Many philosophers have plugged away at answering life's questions, such as: What am I? Why am I here? What is the meaning of life? What would truly make me happy? The answer to these questions is not something material. Many seem to be searching for it.

Another word for Self Realization is Enlightenment. Is Enlightenment possible? Most people don't consider the possibility of Enlightenment as a reality. I didn't. "That's for Buddha and Jesus and people like that, but not me" they think. Actually in this day and age, it is very possible for people to gain a higher level of consciousness and experience profound spiritual clarity. Many are catching a glimpse of Unity consciousness. This may sound preposterous or just not important, but it truly involves your life every day. Why do things happen the way they do? Why are there so many problems, so much suffering in the world? What is the cause of suffering?

We will all experience tragedy in our lifetimes. Pain, death, disaster and loss are an innate part of life. They are inevitable. How well equipped will we be to handle and understand what is happening? How will these events be viewed? Will they be experienced as a deep wound in our being, or as an opportunity? All of Life is perfectly choreographed to help us grow, succeed and be happy, even events we interpret as negative. Imagine how much easier life would be with further understanding and acceptance. It would be enlightening, wouldn't it?

How do I go about it? There are many routes to Self Realization and many tools to help one along the path. One great tool at our disposal is that of a genuine teacher. To align or study with someone who is Self Realized can be a more direct route. Those who teach are at varying levels of understanding and very few are actually at the level that is most helpful. It is important to align with the highest understanding possible. A teacher is an invaluable guide on the path, as they have already traveled the journey you are embarking on. They know the routes with potholes and the tourist traps and can help you circumvent them. They can help you understand what you are experiencing, or where you may be stuck. For most, this is much quicker than going it alone. Just being in their presence many times reveals one's own answers. Their energetic field is more complete and fills in the blanks, so to speak, in our awareness.

Of great assistance is to read books by teachers that contain higher Truths. Great benefit can come from reading the words of someone who has completed the earth path and is free from the suffering of the world. Books provide access to many different teachers and ideas from different vantage points. It can open one to new and more effective ways to look at life or oneself.

Meditation is helpful on the journey of Self Realization as a means to calm the overactive mind and help one to be present. It can help us gain a clearer perspective. Meditation can allow one to open to a higher level of consciousness and have spiritual experiences more readily.

The enlightenment process also involves the intent to be a more loving person, to be more kind, generous and less self-concerned. It involves the understanding that happiness is not going to come from a thing and a looking deeper for happiness beyond the material gain and pleasures that the world offers. Who do you know that is eternally satisfied with a big house or the fastest car? That kind of happiness is fleeting. It is much more fulfilling to build relationships and promote peaceful, healthy lives. To do things for others to demonstrate one's love or help them in some way can bring fulfillment. Think how much better our quality of life would be if everyone were helping others and we all worked together? It would be amazing. If you would like to live that way, why not start now?

Any and all of these practices can be beneficial. In the end, understanding is granted by Grace when it is granted. Everyone's path is different, but as the Buddha said: "There are only two mistakes one can make along the road to Truth; not going all the way, and not starting."

AUTHOR'S JOURNEY

As a small child, I wondered what the point to all this was. I was the kid who asked the questions like "Who am I?" or "Why are we here?" I wanted to understand the purpose of this life. There was so much discontent from the lack of answers that I became depressed and full of despair. Life seemed quite pointless. I became weak and kind of sickly, as if there was little will to live. I was in a delicate condition for the majority of my younger life.

In college, it hit me that I would soon enter a world I did not understand and felt unprepared for. I became very ill to the point the doctors were unable to treat me. I turned to alternative healing and began to study holistic health and get better. As I embraced principles of life giving substances, my body was responding. I had two beautiful children by natural childbirth. I also began to learn about spiritual and intuitive healing. I learned many techniques that helped me gain more understanding and control over my body, my energy and indirectly, my life. After getting my doctorate degree in holistic nutrition, I practiced alternative health and nutrition for 10 years. Then life shifted.

I had what most would consider the comfortable suburban housewife's life: a home with two kids and a husband with a good income. But - I was still very unhappy. I was depressed and living in what seemed to be an unconscious dream world. I was unable to show much love to my husband and kids. I knew there had to be something more. I didn't know that my life wasn't the problem, but rather my perception of life. The suffering that came from not knowing the answers to my lifelong questions was all-encompassing. Why in the world am I here? What REALLY matters? Others didn't seem to share my interests or priorities. Life as I knew it was insane, fear-based and hopeless on the deepest internal level. I felt totally lost. A personal crisis of sorts erupted, as well as a divorce. I was in search of Truth.

So honestly seeking, I was gently and unknowingly pointed toward Truth. My soul was resistant, but excited on some level, and finally I committed to the task of becoming 'Enlightened', whatever that meant. I began to study Enlightenment with Brian Nager of RevealingTruthNow.com and immediately things began to shift. I started putting my life back together. Physical healing and healing on other levels became apparent and I was grateful. I had many amazing spiritual experiences as well as glimpses of extreme peace, love and bliss. Realizing this is what I had been waiting for, I lapped it up. I studied and read every bit of information from teachers of Truth I could get my hands on. I went to retreats with enlightened teachers. I implemented all I learned on a daily basis and incorporated this attitude into my life. Every moment was devoted to discovering what Truth is.

During this part of the journey, I had many amazing experiences that I never knew were even possible. The Peace that ensued is beyond words. For all of this, I feel immense relief and gratitude. After several months of intense personal work, a small shift occurred. It was so subtle, but forever life changing in perspective. All was indeed One. The day that followed was one of completion – all my questions had been answered and all problems dissolved. But I found this was the beginning, not the end. This is where the journey really began. This was 5 years ago, and my journey continues. Now my life is more and more devoted to Truth and loving and helping others. As the old persona is discarded, the True Self is revealed. One's True Self is all of Ourselves. It is pure potential of whatever we can imagine it to be. The path can bring freedom and joy and relief from pain, suffering and fear. It is my hope and intention for all that they find their healing and joy and all the amazing and wonderful things life offers.

Stuck in the Box

Day after day we go about our lives, not questioning them. We do as we're told; we jump on our hamster wheels and run. Where are we going? It is a huge blind spot in the human race: we do not know what we are. We have no idea of what we are capable of. The fact is that almost everyone is experiencing suffering because of a thought, conscious or not. This is the thought that we are limited – by *something*. One becomes a victim in this state. We just don't know there is another way. We as a people are ignorant about what life is about and what kind of life is possible. It is like playing a game without knowing the rules first. We are on the board game of life and we keep moving forward, but we don't know what for. Aren't you curious?

Most people's lives are ruled by what they think of as outside factors. They may believe they are at the mercy of the world, God, others, circumstance, disease, etc. The majority do not think they are infinite or eternal. They don't know there is more out there. This leads to a helpless, victim-oriented society wondering what they can get, and blaming others for problems, instead of focusing on what they do have and what they can create. This seems to be a major area of ignorance in the world that is very painful for many. It is a way we trap ourselves in our own suffering. It is not fun to feel powerless.

This is why it is so important to think outside the "box." A box is a structure with walls, and when you're in it, you can only see what is on the inside. It is a set of rules, beliefs or a way of living that says "this is how it works", but what it really says is "This is the only way it works." The walls of a box do not include all options, and by virtue of being walls, omit everything outside the box as being a potential solution. A box is a structure of limitation. How many of you are in a box? In mom or dad's box, in society's box, in a friend or loved one's box, your very own box.....how many of you don't know or haven't even thought about it? When people are unhappy or unfulfilled, it is because they are in a box. They have unknowingly limited themselves to a certain perception or viewpoint. They think, "This is just how I am. This is how the world is – I am stuck with this." They are focused on a viewpoint and rarely if ever re-evaluate their viewpoint. This viewpoint maybe borrowed and developed from others, or from experience - usually a combination of these. This falsely placed limitation on one's being creates a sense of longing and urgency to see outside the box. This situation can become quite uncomfortable.

When one is in a box, they cannot imagine a different reality. They certainly cannot imagine an infinite one and may not even be familiar with this possibility. We are infinite beings trying to function in a limited way. It cramps our style. A being with infinite potential when placed in a limited environment feels like a caged animal: they can get discouraged, aggressive, depressed, and long to be released to their true, infinite nature. It is only natural. We want to be free to be what we are.

So, what if we turn and look into what we are as that boundless potential… We can choose to combat this ignorance about our inherent nature with our God given curiosity to investigate what we are. We can choose to look into what we don't know about ourselves and the world around us. What is really true? What are you allowing to limit you? If you are indeed infinite, then this limitation you experience cannot be real. Find ways to deny its validity in your life and you will experience a fuller, more peaceful life. This is what is meant by Self Infinity - a state of autonomy in which one is free from the bondage of illusion or false understanding. This is what this book is about.

We are infinite beings trying to function in a limited way. It cramps our style.

Infinite Potential

From the time we are little, we are taught that we are limited, both directly and indirectly. Often, we unknowingly work off of information or even systems of information created by fear. We hear warnings from adults: "Careful! You might get hurt." The worry or fear programs us and perpetuates itself. At the time of learning or programming, we might remember feeling fear in the room, or noticing how others were acting. We subconsciously become that same energy when similar circumstances arise throughout our lives. This shows how our environment and our limited perceptions affect what we become.

Then we see other people - a select few - align with higher divine truths exceeding man-made concern and perception. They have gone outside the box and said "I am not defined by this. It isn't true for me – I feel my potential is unlimited." In doing so, they create their reality from a different place – one of openness, power and joy. To recognize one's infinite power is to harness and unleash it. Doing so creates amazing results and a sense of freedom. Our infinite potential is where our strength is. It allows one to experience a spirit of enthusiasm and creativity. The mind and emotions are invaluable tools that have their place in helping us function efficiently, but they are limited tools that cannot rule over the Universal domain, which is Infinite.

You may have heard the term "personal power." This refers to how powerful an individual feels and acts. It is common in our world today to see attitudes of helplessness and resignation. At times one may feel powerless. To the naked eye, one's circumstances may look bleak. But we are unaware of something important - we are unaware of our abilities and potential as unlimited beings. We are unaware of our infinite potential to change and grow. And, maybe most importantly, we are unaware of the vast assortment of basic tools we have at our disposal.

More and more, I am amazed at our capabilities. Just because we are alive, we have infinite potential. We just didn't know this. We thought we were in charge of fixing all our problems, rather than shifting our focus. We thought we had to take whatever hand we were dealt. Now we choose to be the dealer. Why not think big? What I notice is, the more I hold the idea of infinite potential in my thoughts, the more powerful and capable I become. Not in a self-serving or egoic sense, but rather just as fact. And, as I hold this Truth about capability in mind, I see it actually manifest around me. The first key is to believe it about yourself - believe you are infinitely enabled and powerful. Just try it on. The power I am talking about actually erases problems, erases negatives. It is the Source of Power Itself. This power is not mysterious or far away – it is our very nature. In this way you do not gain power, you realize you *are* power.

EXERCISE:

Make a list of things you would like to do or have in your life. Then see what excuses you are making that keep these form happening. Ex: I don't have time, I'm not good enough, I can't afford it, etc.

What I want: Excuse:

_____

_____

_____

_____

_____

_____

_____

_____

_____

_____

_____

_____

_____

Affirm: "I am, I can, I will. I am helped and guided at all times"

TRUST

Trust is reliance on a person or thing. Trust is key in one's progress on the spiritual path. One can cultivate Trust or faith in oneself, in others, in teachers, and in the Source, from which all comes. If you do not trust a teacher or the process, the distrust or doubt blocks or limits the way in which you receive healing and further growth. If Truth is light coming through a window, suspicion or lack of trust create a film or covering which allows less light to shine through.

For instance, if you are led to work with a valid teacher or read a particular book and feel they are positive in nature and resonate with you, then accept them fully. If you take the teacher's advice halfheartedly, are critical of him/her and judge what he/she says, you are not open to the full Truth. Maybe you are only OK with the teacher's advice if it is what you think it should be, or if the teacher uses words familiar to you. If the teacher resonates with you, treasure that connection and let it soak into your being. This is what trust is. It's likely you will not get nearly as much out of the relationship if you are judging the teacher or the teachings. You can use your discretion and common sense to see if what is discussed rings true or is coming from a loving, positive space or not. Discretion and common sense are helpful faculties. Fear and doubt are not.

If you find yourself not accepting something, find out why – is it because it doesn't make sense? That may be because it is a higher truth than you have previously known and it doesn't yet make sense in your old framework. You are used to something different, more limited. That's the point – to open to the new. Let the information in and give it a trial run. Then you can discard it later if it doesn't work for you. If you find the new idea challenges a concept that you live by, examine your old concept and see why you hold it to be so dear. Could your concept be outdated? As long as the new concept is positive in nature, you will be moving forward, even if it is just different from the way you viewed things in the past. The new concept still allows for expansion of your consciousness. You have nothing to lose but old thoughts and ideas.

Trust Poem

Let go.
Free fall,
Fully trusting
Into the vastness that you are.
To be fearful of Oneself is insane.
Why would one resist themselves?
Once the Truth is known,
That you are the Divinity that you seek,
what is there to fear?
Trust and know All is Love.
You know this and it resonates
Because it is you.

Chapter 2 – How-to

The Integrated Path

How does one integrate spiritual practice into daily life? Most people see daily life and spiritual practice as separate. Prayer is for Sunday mornings or specific designated times where spiritual practice or ritual takes place separate from the grind of daily life. The rituals and words happen and then all goes back to what it was before – status quo. This is normal for most of the world. Even spiritual seekers have their set of practices such as reading, or prayer and meditation, but may separate this routine from the rest of daily activity. Occasionally, one may feel so drawn to the Path that they give up their current way of life and retreat to a mountain top or ashram to seek Truth. This type of isolation from everyday life isn't necessary or practical for everybody, even though they may feel a strong pull to go within and find the Truth.

One reason it can be difficult to integrate spirituality into modern life is that the two often contradict each other. In life, the majority of our thoughts and daily activities are based on getting what we want or think we need. The mind is often filled with self interest and survival oriented thinking. For instance, most people go to work not because they love to give, but because they have to work in order to survive in the way they have become accustomed. So, life focus is about us and what we want.

Spiritual practices usually encourage the opposite – generosity and selflessness. The spiritual ideal is unity and giving - not fighting for the best parking space. Because of this dichotomy, merging our lives with our spiritual practices is not always easy and can cause confusion and internal conflict. But, by adding higher virtues to our way of living, old ways can change for the better. Gradually, the self-focused and security-centered lifestyle changes to one that is peaceful and promotes all of life. Our lives become a sacred space we respect and for which we are thankful.

Since our American society has lived with the sacred mostly missing, it is very important to reintegrate higher values. Life offers one great opportunities at every turn to develop virtues like patience, kindness, thoughtfulness, etc. It is still very helpful to consciously reflect on these virtues, to take time in meditation, to take small breaks for silence, and to be present with what is occurring. Doing these kinds of practices while living one's life will help bring further understanding.

As one begins to be present in each moment, being grateful for the gift of life, every moment becomes a relationship with the Divine. Daily life becomes infused with the Awe of Creation. Each moment is a gift of Grace, and in our fog, we are missing it. We think of our lives as mundane or ordinary, rather than allowing each experience or situation to be a direct encounter with God.

Being present in our life situation is a spiritual practice that can be done anywhere, anytime. If a situation is experienced as unpleasant or uncomfortable, one can use the experience to grow from by watching one's reaction to the situation. It is really an opportunity that lets one know one's current level of acceptance. Lack of acceptance blinds one to reality and accounts for much of human suffering.

To consciously grow toward unity, one can work on accepting what Is and use life circumstances to align with a higher level of peace, love or any of the pure aspects of Reality. For instance, if your goal is to be more compassionate, you would look for every opportunity to be compassionate every day. In this way, life becomes a spiritual practice.

APPLICATION

Here is a more in-depth look at applying truths in daily life. By being alert to the current situation and assessing one's reaction to it, we can change our reality from the unconscious one we've been living to a consciously created one. If we don't consciously decide how we would like to live, we will get whatever the default is. Life will be just whatever shows up… not "Wow, Amazing!" This is where we find victim consciousness, where one feels one is helpless in the situation, not the creator of the situation.

When we are unconscious in our lives, it is like getting in the car and starting to drive without knowing where we are going and not looking at a map. When we are conscious or awake in our lives, we are interested in what we truly are. We are interested in being the fullness of that, utilizing our potential. We can then align with a teacher or informational guidelines to create amazing lives with purpose and passion.

A great way to use the information we learn is to apply it to situations in daily life. With everything you do, look at why you do it. Keep a running dialog about it in your head. Question your daily activities. Why do you do what you do? How does it relate to what really matters? If what you are doing doesn't align with what matters to you, change what you are doing. For instance, if you don't like your job, are stressed out and your health is suffering, then this will be motivation to change the situation. You may now decide what matters is your health and experiencing more joy from life.

Another technique is to examine our attachment to material objects. What does one really want when one buys and consumes material possessions? Is it comfort or entertainment? One can use these opportunities present in life to look at where one *wants* and feels unfulfilled. Is it food, objects, or people one wants, and feels will make them happy, more complete or add to their current experience? Do material objects provide ultimate fulfillment? All are disappointing in the long run, because they are temporary and do not satisfy eternally. One can have anything, just not be attached to the thing as providing happiness. Happiness is an inside job. It is available all the time as a choice.

One might find a positive affirmation helpful, or a reminder like "I am fulfilled and complete" or "There is an infinite vibration of happiness available at all times." When situations arise that would typically involve personal greed or self-gratification, one can affirm and strengthen their awareness of eternal happiness by thinking of others first. It can be an opportunity to grow by serving others.

If one is not feeling that the spiritual path applies in the current situation, One can look closely and be very honest with oneself. The ego can be tricky when we want what we want and we can convince ourselves it is really best to have it, or that we deserve it.

Continue to analyze your current choices. Rely on this process throughout the day, watching what you do, say and think. Work on this in your mind and on paper. This will help to clean up your lifestyle to match what you want to be and have. A more lasting and permanent happiness will be revealed.

Why do you do what you do? How does it relate to what really matters?

TOOLS FOR THE PATH

It is helpful to have some guidelines and tools for the path. You will know if the tools are right for you, as you are the one who knows you best. There is not one set way or technique that is the only way. Our inspiration and understanding can come from anywhere, sometimes from surprising sources.

There are many tools that are beneficial, each addressing a different angle or aspect. Many of these just involve being aware or mindful in daily life. All practices work best when there is a high level of commitment or devotion to the Truth. When one is sincere and truly wants to discover and understand, growth comes quickly.

PRACTICAL STEPS AND PRACTICES

There are many approaches to the path and not all approaches work for all individuals. It is helpful to try a variety of practices to help one learn to be still, connect, deprogram and heal. Some practices to consider are: Studying Foundational Truth, Self Inquiry, Surrender, Meditation and Positive Focus. Let's look at each one and how to apply them…..

1. Foundational Truth

What is True? How do you know? Everyone has a set of beliefs about what is true. These beliefs are built on a foundation of some sort. It may be something we heard or were taught. If may be something we formulated from experiences we have had. Whatever the origin, the mind uses these concepts to build a foundation. This foundation supports the paradigm by which we live.

If one is seeking the ultimate Truth, one is looking for answers. What one wants and gets used to in the physical world is concrete, objective answers. At this time on earth, there is such diversity in thought. There are many different ideas and concepts about what reality is, what God is, and how one should live one's life. Some of these ideas are more loving, life-promoting and peaceful than others. And to a great extent, one can choose what one thinks. One can choose what they will hold as important, as valuable, as true. This becomes the foundation. Whether one realizes it or not, One has laid a foundation from one's thoughts and beliefs. Once one realizes there is a conscious choice, one can discard any beliefs that do not support infinite potential and weaken one's foundation. Why would one choose a reality that includes ignorance and suffering? Those who seek personal growth and betterment of the world around them can begin to implement positive choices and build a strong foundation. Doing so sets in motion a powerful intention and builds the momentum to create amazing and miraculous things. Positive choices allow a level of fulfillment that one cannot get through other means.

To learn about Foundational Truths, it is helpful to study from the great minds on the planet. Foundational Truths are found in the writings and/or teachings of those who know Oneness firsthand and are at a high level of knowingness. These teachers are aware of our True Nature and can guide us toward this level of Oneness. Usually these Truths are summed up in simple words such as:

All is Love.

All is One.

God is All.

I Am.

When Truths like these are seen and not fully understood, it is hard not to dismiss them or take them lightly. Sure, it makes sense, but do you *truly* experience your life that way? Try to check the concepts for yourself with an open mind. These truths are so literal and profound, it is best to sit with them awhile and let them sink in. Spend time with these truths, repeat them, feel them, and ponder them. These truths can form an unshakeable foundation for peace and freedom from suffering.

For instance, let's look at the truth "God is All." This is a theme in most major religions and philosophies around the globe. It appears in phrases such as: God is all encompassing, omnipresent, immanent and transcendent, etc. Since this concept is found in many cultures over time, we reason that the concept "God is All" is held in common among most people. The notion may resonate with you enough for you to look deeper. The vibrational or contextual truth can be felt behind the words. You may agree that yes, on some level, this makes sense or rings true. You can confirm it with some innate level of knowingness. The idea is for you to dig into it more and more until it is understood and realized fully. What does it mean to you? The more one seeks to know Truth, the more it reveals itself and becomes reality as What Is. There is then experiential evidence of the Truth and one knows it to be one's reality beyond doubt – one can see it in one's daily life.

As one thinks of truth throughout the day, one might start like this: "Wow, look at those beautiful flowers. *God is ALL*..... hhhhmmm......Well, I can see how the essence of beauty and of all life would be from God's hand....OK.....so all is *from* God..... well, where is God exactly ....is God omnipresent/everywhere? Then how could God not be present always in all things? One could go on and on until an "aha" brings further understanding. Keep looking, the truth is......*everywhere*. When looking around at how the world works, how timing and synchronicity happen, how things unfold perfectly when seen from a larger scale, we begin to see the presence of Grace. The mundane becomes amazing.

Spend time with these truths, repeat them, feel them, ponder them. These truths can form an unshakeable foundation for Peace and freedom from suffering.

2.   Self Inquiry

Self inquiry is the digging into your deeper being to answer some of your unanswered questions. If you are interested in Truth, you will be naturally drawn to find it by questioning reality. Question everything in your path. Why do you do what you do? What is your motive? Is it selfish or selfless? Keep a journal and write about the things in your life. Compare your thoughts and experiences to an ideal, such as a foundational truth. Ask yourself a question on paper that you want to know the answer to, and have it answered from a higher, more truthful perspective. This requires self honesty.

Example: What is God? What is Love? What is the truth about _____? Write it down. You may think you already have an answer, but be willing to release old concepts and see what new information appears.

Develop a relationship with your "Self."
- This is an intimate and personal understanding that develops from continual and practiced communication with the inner, or Higher Self.
- When looking for higher information, one must ask a higher source than one is currently accessing. All that is needed is the intention to do so. You can use a source you know and trust to be an expression of Wisdom and Truth, the higher the better. This would include spiritual teachers and any/all liberated beings.
- Become familiar with your intuition. Get used to the feelings, signals, and ways that you receive information and messages.
- Ways to access the higher levels may include talking/praying, listening/hearing, knowing/trusting gut feelings, meditation/ visualizations, pendulum/dowsing, and journaling/writing. All of these are ways of asking for a higher Truth to be revealed.

- The relationship with Self is always established in the form of asking, or from a place of humility, such as "I really don't know, but am open to suggestions." Be teachable.
- An important ingredient is self honesty. If you are not completely honest with yourself, you are kidding yourself, and wasting your time. Ask yourself "What is my motive or agenda? What do I *really* want to get out of this?"

Inquire into your own life issues
- When something surfaces in your life that you would like to deal with more effectively or you would like deeper insight into (which might be everything,) use a method of asking noted above. Writing is more effective than "thinking it through," as it allows one to go deeper and have more complete thoughts. This is important. Try writing if you have not. This can take your processing to the next level.
- Use mindfulness on the small stuff all day long to unravel why your life is the way it is. Look at what you think and do.
- A key to growth is to be willing to scrutinize everything – belief systems, identity, patterns, habits, attachments, aversions, etc.

Inquire into foundational truth (see Foundational Truth, pg 16) and why it is true for you.
- Use your understanding of Foundational Truth to put your current issue or situation in a truthful perspective. Take everything back to the foundational level and put in the context of Truth. The highest conceptual understanding one holds will help foster an experience of that understanding. The reason one does the inquiry process in the first place is to have less suffering and realize a higher way of thinking and doing. The new understanding can only be as high as the thought or feeling that is the foundation. Why limit yourself?

Reach for the stars…reach as high as you can. Reaching with the mind helps to pull it up higher.

3.   Process of Surrender

Surrender is what happens inside when one sees the pointlessness in the struggle and stops struggling. This usually happens when the mind has enough new information that it lets go of an old concept, as it sees that there is a better way and that the old concept clearly causes suffering. It no longer sees the validity hanging onto the past action or thought. Two forms of surrender are release and acceptance. Release is a way of getting rid of old issues or clearing blocks from your awareness. The old way of being no longer serves a purpose, so it begins to leave. What actually leaves might be an unuseful thought, feeling or action. Recognizing it as being unhelpful is all that is needed to begin the releasing process.

Acceptance is allowing and fully loving the situation or issue. Not rejecting that aspect of self or life, but affirming its place in the ongoing process and embracing it as necessary and useful. Not just tolerating it, but able to feel positive towards it. Looking for the positive in all….it is always there. We are trained to see and feel the negative. But remember, the process is that we go through in life is Perfect as is. We are the ones not accepting this fact.

Surrender to Divine Will is the deepest form of surrender and is all that is needed for the path. Surrender dissolves all problems one has with reality.

4.   Meditation

Why meditate? Meditation has many commonly noted benefits, including reduction of stress and anxiety, and revitalizing the mind and body. It is also known for improving concentration and focus, increasing learning ability and memory, and raising self awareness. Emotionally, reported results include the experience of more tolerance, harmony, confidence, and an overall positive attitude. Meditation is commonly used by athletes to increase performance and focus. And spiritually, meditation is often used to help open one to a greater Presence or experience of Grace, to allow a higher reality to come through. Having personal experiences in meditation can raise one's understanding and facilitate spiritual growth. Although many religions include meditation, it not part of a particular belief system. Meditation does not require a lifestyle change, does not have to be time-consuming, and can be learned by anyone regardless of age or level of education. It is you, alone with yourself. And as it turns out, you are very good company.

In today's world, we have set very fast paced, multi-tasking roles for ourselves. This tends to overload the senses and body systems that interpret stimuli. The brainwaves are more active, which can throw off the balance of mind and body. When the brain is overactive and stressed, a person's equilibrium is compromised. This creates an ideal environment for many common imbalances to manifest, such as attention deficit disorder and hyperactivity, obsessive/compulsive disorders, headaches, fast talking, and anxiety. Meditation techniques help the mind become calm and focused. With meditation, much more internal peace and clarity are available for a person to access. Meditation can also balance the brainwaves, allowing higher awareness and function. The mind works better when it is still and alert, not foggy or full of fast-paced thoughts. With meditation, the mind becomes an empty container ready for input from the Divine.

MEDITATIONS

Below are two simple meditations that can be practiced at almost any stage of the path for general clearing and awareness. Begin by practicing meditation at least10 minutes a day. Pick a technique and try it for at least two weeks.

Meditation 1: Clearing & Breath Awareness

Begin by sitting comfortably in a chair with the spine comfortably straight. Arrange your hands on your legs or in your lap. Bring the attention to your breathing. Just be the observer of the breath. You don't have to change it, just watch what naturally happens. Relax your abdominal muscles. Follow the breath in and out. Allow this to be effortless as you witness the flow. No need to control any part of the process, just observe. Now as you breathe in, see this breath as a white or gold healing breath. Breathe in fully accepting the healing energy all the way down into the body. When you exhale, breathe out any black, gray or brown energy, whatever color you see is perfect. This can represent anything old or stagnant that you wish to release. Breathe in the white or gold…..breathe out the old gray or brown air. Now breathe out any energy from your day, any problems or situations you encountered. Repeat this until you feel you've released the day. Next, breathe out and release any lists of tasks to do. Again, do this until you feel the process is complete. Then, breathe out any energies or issues you have with anyone. Just intend to release them. Breathe out any thoughts that arise. Thought doesn't allow you to be present- right here, right now. Just be aware of the breathing. Be awareness itself.

Now start to be aware of your body and the room. Be aware of any sounds. Feel the air touching your skin and the chair under you. Feel your feet on the floor & wiggle your toes. Wiggle your fingers as you feel the body and slowly, when you are ready, open your eyes.

Mediation 2: Sit with Yourself

Just sit with yourself. Do nothing. Can you do nothing? For how long? Just enjoy Being. See what you are. Allow understanding to come to you without reaching for it. It will reveal itself to you. This is a helpful practice to incorporate into life. Just to Be, with a willing and open attitude can allow more understanding than to do an active practice. Be willing to observe what you are, as if you've never met yourself. If you haven't done this before, it may take getting used to. At first, it may take a little while to release all the thoughts in mind, and this is new and unfamiliar ground if your mind is not usually empty. The mind is a processing machine and wants input to process, but just like everything else, it does better when given a little rest.

If anything comes into the mind, notice it and watch it come and go, not paying attention to the content. You may hear a running dialog such as: "This is boring. What am I supposed to do? Am I doing it right? I think I forgot turn off my phone....." Be patient as this clears out. It will clear eventually. Gradually increase the time you sit with yourself.

Begin by practicing meditation 10 minutes a day. Pick a technique and try it for at least two weeks.

5. Positive Focus

A positive focus or good attitude can be a large part of the equation. Teachings about the Law of Attraction are prevalent. Learn to use it in a Universal and unity based context so the best for all can be manifested, not just for personal gain.

POSITIVE FOCUS AND THE LAW OF ATTRACTION

Remember the analogy of "the glass is half full"? It is important to remember the power of a positive outlook, attitude and thinking. Some people have an affinity toward a positive outlook. Others have to work more to cultivate it. On the spiritual path, it is important to learn to live it. It may be our most powerful tool, in that the moment all is seen in a positive light, negative can't exist.

In this world there is duality, meaning opposites like night and day, dark and light, empty and full, etc. Duality already assumes there is a positive and a negative. But the foundational truth of "All is Love" knocks the concept of duality out of the water. If All is Love, there can never be non-love. There is never a negative. This means All is Love, no exceptions.

If there is only positive, there is nothing to get rid of, release, or fight against. The whole dualistic paradigm falls away as negativity is seen to be an illusion. A negative thought invites a problem and its friends: worry, anxiety and uncertainty. When we have a problem, we tend to focus on it to try and fix it, or we worry about how it will affect us. This problem-focus continues to fuel the problem. The attention the problem gets affirms its reality. By shifting our attention away from the negative to positive thinking, we can turn the problem around into a positive. It is only our reaction to what is happening that can be a negative. Reality is happening "As Is". One person might interpret the events as positive while another might experience them as filled with suffering.

For instance, if it is raining, one person might say: "Ugh, I hate rain. It is so gray and dreary and I always get my feet wet." Another might experience it this way "Wow, it's raining…..how beautiful. I love rainy days, they are so relaxing and everything seems clean and renewed." The rain is the same, it doesn't change - only the viewpoint changes.

We can choose how we view life's situations. We can choose how we react. If we only trust that everything is perfect the way it is as an expression of Love and do nothing else, the results will be phenomenal. All expressions, feelings, experiences, thoughts, etc. can only be Love if it is seen that Love is All that Is. God *is* the process. God is Life. Try turning your positives into negatives. You might like it.

If you have been paying attention lately, you may have seen someone talking about the law of attraction in the media. We have been pointed toward this universal law as a tool. The Law of Attraction states that we create and attract the things in our lives. Our energies attract like energies. Negative attracts negative and positive attracts positive.

So, we can use this information to become what we want. The quickest way to do this is to hold a positive focus while cleaning out old baggage, patterns and hidden beliefs to uncover our naturally positive Self.

EXERCISE:

Make a list of anything "negative" or problematic about yourself or your life. Then rewrite it as a positive or opposite statement. If you have a hard time finding anything positive, think of someone who might not be as fortunate in that area and then feel the gratitude for your situation.

Example - Negative: I do not have enough money
Positive: I am thankful for the money I **do** have! I am capable of attracting more good things into my life.

_____
_____
_____
_____
_____
_____
_____

CHAPTER 3 – THE PROCESS

TRANSCENSION

In the online dictionary www.freedictionary.com , *Transcend* is defined as: **1.** To pass beyond the limits of. **2.** To be greater than, as in intensity or power; surpass. **3.** To exist above and independent of.

When something is transcended, one has passed beyond it to something new. If one is not experiencing the highest level of awareness or highest Reality that is possible, they have to transcend or release the current level to move on. What seems real now is only one possibility or idea of what's out there to experience. One might recognize "This is not the fullest expression of love possible." When this arises, one can choose to surrender the current experience and ask for a higher reality to experience (see self inquiry section, pg 19). It is like going up steps to a more positive reality. To transcend limitation, this process is continually repeated. Do this without getting stuck or staying in any one experience.

Road Blocks

A funny thing happens when one wakes up to life or becomes conscious. When the decision is made to move forward consciously, a lot of issues can come up and seem to thwart the process. In fact, it can seem like everything but what we are asking for shows up. This might be the point at which a lot of people give up. But understanding that this is part of the process may allow one to continue.

Often the process goes like this: when we decide to change our lives, we set something powerful in motion. We continue to move forward on our path, but with our eyes open. As these changes occur, all of our limitations that kept old patterns in place surface to be released. This is a purification process - we begin to clean house. This can serve as a clarifying and refining stage. It can fine tune someone and strengthen them to be their best. The obstacles that arise can actually be the stepping stones needed to make you exactly what you want to be. It is really what you've asked for, in process. Remember, the layout of this Plan is perfect. There are no flaws. This is the kind of Faith needed to allow the Divine to work through you and manifest your dreams. So, knowing about this process can keep one from being discouraged. You are just clearing out any obstacles so you can experience your true Self. You are asking for personal transformation, which isn't always glamorous or comfortable in the beginning.

Resistance & Fear

On the journey, sometimes we hesitate, stand still, or even try to turn back. We may feel there is not enough information, skill or courage to move forward. It is not yet clear what will unfold or how. Inner conflict can result. There is a part of us that thinks it would be best to continue, yet another part of us is unsure. Until the resistance is out of the way, we cannot trust the path fully and validate it as true. *Something* is still blocking the full understanding, or we would trust it.

What is resistance? Resistance is anything that blocks the complete Knowledge and Love of God. Resistance can be in many forms. It is commonly seen in the form of uncertainty and fear, which keeps us from moving forward. The resistance can be fear of the unknown. How do I know? When will I know? We cannot ever know the unknown. That is what faith is. Whatever is keeping you from believing in the part with forward vision is what we can work with. As the resistant part gets smaller and the forward motion part gets bigger, we will have less dragging the ground and more movement. So we chip away at the resistance with our tools. We work to release it. Often, we don't have to decipher and sort back through it, unearth pain and experience it all over again. It can be a simple awareness or recognition, that's all it takes. It doesn't matter what it is, let it go. It's old, it's over. You don't need it. If it is blocking you, *Throw It Out*.

Sometimes it is a new way of looking at an old issue that allows us to release it. We may have to revisit things that are ingrained and need a little prying to come loose. This process may require help at certain times; is often very rewarding and brings about fantastic change. It transforms the story you've been telling yourself into one without problems. The story is only old ways of thinking, a dream that you've dreamed too long.

Believing the dream is the block to knowingness. The dream is our own version of the way things "should" go. We want to be who we want to be; who we think we "should" be. This is a fictional world created in the mind to feel safe and in control - the world of "Should". We spend much of our time trying to make this world happen, regardless of what it costs us. But it costs us our Peace. This is not the authentic world, the authentic Self, but a dream world. Look past the dream. It is the resistance to what's eternal. The Truth is who you really are, right now.

Whether you like or don't like yourself or the world is irrelevant. They exist. To be willing to look squarely at yourself, and see what Is. The trick is to be OK with who you really are, to Love that person. Accept what Is as the truth, with no judgment good or bad. Full acceptance of the world and yourself is what heals the pain. Love heals all.

After step one, there are actually functional reasons to make changes. Not out of greed or vanity, but because the change would improve function or quality of life. It would improve the life of others. Then be OK with the decision to change it and do it. Be OK with the process. The best motive is to always do what is best for the Whole. That is all you can do. You can act on what you know and the information you've been given. They are all you've got. So, move forward in faith. You may not get what you expected, but it is closer to what you are truly looking for.

Resistance is anything that blocks the complete Knowledge and Love of God.

WHEN THE GOING GETS ROUGH

When the going gets rough, what can we do? The first thought is usually "how do I get rid of the problem or smooth this out as quickly as possible?" Although this is what we think we want, we don't want to get rid of the value or purpose of the things that happen in our lives. We want to learn to be at peace in any situation and see its value. There are no problems - this is just the way a situation is perceived mid-crisis. Everything that happens to us has a distinct purpose. There are tools available to make the process smoother. Let's look at what our tools are and how to use them, so we can begin to move toward a more positive experience in any situation.

1.   Make a list.

Simply make a list of what you're feeling or what's bothering you. You may not even be sure exactly, so write it down. Just to clarify what you are feeling can help a lot. A list might look something like this:

- I feel depressed
- Relationship issues
- Too hard
- Too busy
- Not enough time
- Car problems
- People are mean
- Etc.

Then when it's on paper, all those things can become one thing instead of many. It's just "The List." Sometimes just acknowledging your inner thoughts and feelings will begin to resolve things or you may see something you weren't aware of before. Release all the problems or issues on the list by giving them over to the Universe, Divine Presence or Higher Self to handle for you. You can say something like: "I release all perceived problems now, I give them to God and ask to see the blessings in life." If this doesn't resolve it completely, go to number 2:

2.   Change the subject

If you are really stuck in something icky and it seems to be staying the same or getting worse as you try to look at it, change the subject. You can do this by going for a walk, changing location, or simply just changing what you are doing. If you are inside, go outside, or switch rooms. Engage in a new activity. Take a shower. If you're alone, go out in public, or meet with a friend. Sometimes a change in situation or activity is all that is needed is to stop the downward spiral. If the problem arises again and again, it cannot be avoided and must be addressed in order to understand the cycle and keep it from perpetuating.

3. Be Still

Sometimes everything seems too chaotic or to have so much momentum we don't know how to stop it or break the cycle. This is a good time to call a time-out. Just by choosing to stop what you are doing right then begins the positive change. You become in charge of your life, instead of it having its way with you. Your time out may be 5 minutes, 5 hours or 5 days, but use this time to switch gears. Do anything different than what you were doing. Be still, breathe, meditate, pamper your body, your mind, etc. Take a break, then consciously decide what your next action will be and why. Consciously choose a new course of action. Take your power back.

4. Flip the Switch

A great technique is the "quick flip" or "flipping the switch". Just like flipping on a light switch, we decide to shift our thinking. When you realize you are in your problems and feeling negative, catch yourself before you go down the rabbit hole. Listen to your thoughts without reacting to them, as if you were an objective friend listening. Or, write them down and then flip each one to a positive. See the lesson, message or blessing in each one and be grateful for each. Instead of "I failed", see it as "I know more now and am moving toward success – here it comes!" If things are not going well in your life, focus on helping someone else. Sometimes seeing others have problems makes us feel human or more secure that we are normal and things will work out. Things are usually not as bad as they seem. After doing so, one naturally feels much better about one's problems and may realize "I don't really have any big problems." If someone else's life is going great, one may be so happy for the other person that one forgets about one's own problems. Be positive. Use affirmations. Get enthusiastic, and inspired!

5. The Polar Opposite

We are in a world of opposites. For example: what goes up must come down, right and wrong, black and white, etc. This is the way our mind works. It is helpful to remember that whatever you are experiencing is only one end of a spectrum of experiences you can have. When we hold something in mind, the current experience is magnified so that it feels very real and strong. A technique to shift the focus from the unpleasant thought or experience to a broader view is to think of the opposite. For instance, if you are feeling sad, the opposite is happy. While you are feeling sad, it is hard to convince yourself you are happy, but they are actually opposite ends of the same vibration. With this understanding, we can slide up the scale. Holding the thought "I am happy" in mind and heart, seeking to find the part of you that knows and identifies with "happy" can shift you back to balance.

6. Surrender

When you are not in a place where you can make a list or take time to be still, holding a space of constant surrender or prayer is greatly helpful. Use the situation you are in by being present in it enough to use it as a positive tool. In each moment, give yourself completely to what's happening. Don't avoid feeling or seeing what is truly happening. Give up what you think the outcome should be. Release all expectations of others. Immediately begin asking for Divine intervention. Pray to be a higher expression of Love and mean it. Give yourself fully for the cause. You can ask for guidance, direction, clarity, etc.

THE BEAUTY IN SUFFERING

One day my daughter told me she learned in school that it is very painful for a caterpillar to become a butterfly. This made a big impression on me. I understood something about life in what she shared: that something as amazing and beautiful as a butterfly wasn't always that. It had to go through an uncomfortable process to become what it was. In our experience on earth, we encounter many processes or transformations like this; we can all relate to discomfort as humans. Growth is sometimes painful, sometimes unbearably so, yet here we stand. The depth of suffering is known only to the one in the midst of experiencing it. It is a personal journey we make and we are taught to interpret the process as painful. Our culture abhors discomfort. We are conditioned from infancy to avoid any discomfort and immediately assuage pain, as though experiencing it is not OK. The fear of 'what's happening to me!' or 'what could happen?!' creates a negative experience. One is feeling fear instead of trusting that one is OK.

Usually, we are OK. We are stronger than we think we are. And it is the personal journey through these transformative times that awakens us. I believe pain and discomfort are some of our greatest teachers and that we deny ourselves opportunities when we sweep them under the rug and ignore them. Pain is not always a negative. It is our interpretation of pain that is negative. Sensation is just that – a sensation felt through the senses: physically or mentally/emotionally. It can be used to alert one that there is danger, or that a course correction is in order. Physical pain can act as a guide to help redirect us during the course of our lives. It is to be respected….as is love, or any other gift.

Emotional pain allows us to learn about humility and feel empathy for others. It reminds us we are vulnerable. Next time you feel pain or discomfort of any kind, try just sitting with it a moment. Feel it. Talk to it as if it were a small child by asking it simple questions like "What are you doing here?" Or, "What message do you have for me?" Find its relevancy to your life. It can be a doorway to further wholeness.

In some cultures, life trials and pivotal points are celebrated and used to strengthen one's character. One honors the changes that life brings and may meditate on its significance or take an inner journey to understand oneself further. One such occasion is childbirth. Childbirth is a miraculous occurrence and the pain and intensity are an integral part of the celebration. The pain or sensation can feel strong and powerful, but is not "bad." I have had two children by natural childbirth methods and wouldn't trade the experience for anything. This is LIFE. You miss living when you drugged or cover up what's real.

Choose to be present. This life we've been given is a gift not to be missed. Many would argue that a lot of life's trials don't feel like gifts at the time, but gifts such as illness and pain help us understand the mysteries and master them. This is the same for anything given into one's awareness, whether perceived as a gift or not. How will you choose to perceive the gifts in your life?

It is the personal journey through these transformative times that awakens us… choose to be present. This life we've been given is a gift not to be missed.

CHAPTER 4 – HEALTH AND HEALING

TRUE HEALTH

Complete health is our natural state. True health stems from higher awareness and understanding, as well as proper care of the body, mind, emotions and spirit as aspects of self. The more one realizes the potential for good health to be a Reality, the more one is freed from the illusion of illness to a higher degree. For instance, if one understands that All is One, then it would be conflicting to believe one is affected by something outside of oneself. If there is only One, then there is no "other" to affect them. One cannot believe "other things" are affecting them at the same time as knowing there is only One. In today's society, we are taught to see viruses, bacteria or germs as icky things to be scared of, to avoid and kill.

When one loves all creatures equally, one would love the germs as much as others and know that they have a perfect place in the universe as Divine creation. A person who is Self Realized knows that they actually ARE all of these creatures. The Truth is literal: All *is* ONE. There is only one thing - Love. And Love does not make you sick. It Heals. The closer one is to realizing the illusion of separation and experiencing the fullness of one's being, the more health one experiences.

THE AUTHOR'S HEALING PATH

My path of physical healing in this life has led me through many different ways of thinking and many types of healing modalities, from the traditional to the alternative and downright unusual. I have gone from being a fairly delicate and sickly child to a dysfunctional, ill young adult and now a healthy adult. As my being heals on the deepest of levels, I feel more and more whole, and my physical health displays this.

In college, I became very ill. At first, I went the traditional medical route. Their tests determined nothing was wrong with me, even though I couldn't drive, walk or get out of bed, and slept 18-20 hours a day. Then I went to a chiropractor/homeopath that proceeded to address imbalances with diet, nutrients, herbs and homeopathic remedies. Healing began and natural health revealed a new level of health for me. Then after reaching a certain plateau, the next piece involved healing the energetic systems of my body. Ancient systems of medicine like Chinese acupuncture and Indian Ayurveda are based on such principles. The physical body and mind are influenced by an energetic correlate or integral system that can be assessed, balanced, cleared and healed, revealing higher awareness. I studied many different types of energy healing. This led to learning about lifestyle imbalances and energy expenditure. I was healthier than I had probably ever been, and was experiencing above average health, but there were still occasional bouts of colds or allergies, although rare.

I then began to study Truth with others and read materials that reflected these Truths. I questioned every belief I had that limited me. I questioned the beliefs against the new understanding I was gaining of what Reality is, what God is, what Truth is. My health has improved to an amazing degree. My body's usual limits are surpassed daily in what it can be, do and accomplish. I sleep less and do more with a better attitude.

What am I doing? I have simply searched for the Truth of who I am. I have looked at what made me ill to begin with, not what's out there, but my own thoughts and beliefs. I have found personal clarity from examining foundational truths and continue to learn more as it is a constantly evolving process. I have studied the great teachings of those that transcended this realm and say that doing so is exclusive to none, that all may experience great healing, peace and understanding if they so choose.

Physical Body and Illness

There are many things that affect and influence the health of the physical body. Genetics, karma, stress, toxins, thoughts/ beliefs, emotions, nutrients, and activity level/exercise are many of the variables. We live in a world where things can affect the physical body. The body appears to have limitations and appears to age, degenerate, and also succumb to illness. It is becoming more widely known that our thoughts have a lot to do with the way molecules in our body respond. For instance, when we think pleasant thoughts, our muscles relax and positive brain chemicals are released. The body and the mind are not separate – they are interrelated and inseparable. Much research is being done in the area of mind/body healing – using thoughts to alter the body's level of health. The potential in this arena is phenomenal and wide open.

Healing Messages

Pain and illness can serve as messengers. When we ignore the message, it gets stronger. We interpret this as negative, uncomfortable and keeping us from our daily lives. When in fact, these messages are a part of our lives – not as problems or interferences, but as positive tools to help us to make a change or get us back on course to optimize our lives. This physical guidance system is one of the most helpful tools we have as human beings to help us be happier and healthier. If we listen without judgment to the "message" and chose to feel it instead of deny it, we will find out more about ourselves and the source of the problem. If we cover it up with medications, ignore it hoping it will go away, or try to stop the symptoms rather than find out what the message is, we deny the problem and we deny ourselves.

These messages are a part of our lives – not as problems or interferences, but as positive tools to help us to make a change.

HEALTH BELIEFS: WHAT AFFECTS THE BODY? HOW MUCH?

The amount that the programming of the physical world affects the physical body depends on one's level of awareness or understanding. The programming of the physical world may affect the body in relation to one's belief system. For instance, if one subscribes to the germ theory, they would naturally think that germs 'attack' or 'infect' the body. This is the way most of the modern world is programmed. If one is fearful of getting sick, one's fear can perpetuate getting sick. Holding the negative vibration of fear allows the negative vibration of dis-ease to enter. A huge portion of disease in our world is a disease of unhealthy thoughts.

There is another theory called the biological terrain theory. This theory states that the body's health is dependent on its general condition or internal environment. Thus disease occurs only when the terrain or internal environment of the body is not strong and becomes susceptible to germs. If one believes their body is strong and healthy and can ward off illness, one is less likely to get sick. This is seen when two people are exposed to the same illness and one "catches" it and the other doesn't. The body and mind are more resilient in the person who thinks positively about his/her health than the person who believes germs attack the body and is fearful of catching something.

If this type of thinking is not one's current belief and experience, one can work to cultivate it. Certain exercises and positive affirmations can correct negative thinking and reprogram the mind with healthy thinking. This process will begin to affect the physical body. The mind will tell the body to make strong, healthy cells and a new you will be born. If we believe we are defenseless against the world, we will be. If we believe there are things out there to fear, then we create that reality. The world does this *en masse*.

Could belief systems about germs affect the physical body? Can a person's perception and experience of the world affect how he/she feels? Studies show how lower stress levels and laughter affect the immune response in a positive way (Stuber, et al. 2007). Try a positive approach to life and health, and trust that all is well, even as you deal with the current problems at hand. Commit to this new way of thinking for a period of time and give it a chance to take effect. The results can only be positive.

To develop a positive belief in the perfection of the body and its ability to heal itself, one can release limiting belief systems by using self inquiry to exchange the old belief system for a foundational truth (see practical steps and practices, pg 16) to experience a higher level of health. By doing this process, the person now has a higher understanding of what reality can be and how this relates to the body and health.

Does one believe that sugar is bad for you and veggies make us healthy? That one should expect problems with their health as they age, such as arthritis, poor eyesight, or hearing loss? These are perfect candidates for the self inquiry process. The body is programmable with thought. If one thinks that fifty is old and believes, even subconsciously that "the eyes go at fifty," they are more likely to actually experience it that way. Since the mind thinks poor eyesight at fifty is reality, the body implements the program – and you become what you think. We have noted many variables that affect our health, such as genetics and nutrition, but our thoughts about all of these affect how they manifest in our lives.

There are people with some of the healthiest diets in the world, yet they are stressed out and worried – their thinking is toxic. They may have as many or more health issues as those who are not as health conscious. It seems many people who have always experienced health have put little thought there, as if health is known to be the default or normal and natural state of the body. The body is smart and heals itself on a regular basis, unless we believe otherwise.

Also, one's alignment with collective consciousness is a huge variable and affects the outcome. If one watches a fear-based report on the news about an epidemic or other illness, and believes it to be True, one's consciousness aligns with everyone who believes the same thing. Then, one is aligned with the collective or mass consciousness fear. If a group of people have the same thought, it is much stronger and persuasive than if only one person thinks it. The concept 'there is strength in numbers' applies, in that everyone believing and holding a thought perpetuates it, whether it is negative or positive.

Entertaining a thought based in fear is not the highest choice, and since we know a positive choice exists, why are we not choosing it right now? One can chose to switch gears and hold a positive focus. This helps to create a positive outcome.

Health Beliefs: The body ages, the body can get ill, the body needs to recuperate and detoxify. What are your health beliefs that are limiting you?

EXERCISE:

Make a list of your beliefs about health and illness. Include things that affect your health. Compare these to the foundational truth All is One. Expand on each one – write about why or how your new understanding is true.

My Health beliefs: **Truth as related to All being One:**

EXAMPLE:

1. Germs make people sick   1. My body is inherently strong and healthy. That is it's natural state, as Oneness is already complete and healed. Germs are created and are allowed to exist. They serve a perfect purpose, so I am grateful for their existence, yet choose not to be negatively affected by them.

2. _____   2. _____
3. _____   3. _____
4. _____   4. _____
5. _____   5. _____
6. _____   6. _____
7. _____   7. _____

After completing the list of as many beliefs as one can think of, an affirmation can be used, such as "I choose True Health, not my unhealthy thoughts. I surrender all limited health beliefs." Then visualize or think of the body in perfect health. Picture the body in the mind's eye as each cell is filled with light and health is restored. Take a few minutes to visualize this.

Remember, your health has been a cumulative process throughout your whole life. As one changes their belief systems, things begin to shift, but outward visible changes don't always happen instantaneously. Continue to care for the body properly and shift how you relate to the body as your new awareness strengthens.

DIFFERENT HEALTH PERSPECTIVES

This leads one to question why the body may currently be at a lower level of health when good health is innate. Why do some people catch every cold while others rarely, if ever get sick. Why would one hold a fear-based belief around health - rather than one of hope and positive thinking? My mother used to employ positive thinking techniques if she felt a cold coming on. She would say "I don't have time to get sick. I'm just not going to get sick." She chose to believe the body was strong enough and that she was well. And you know what? It worked. She rarely got sick.

My parents always told me "you can do anything you want." I believed them and took them literally. The foundation of this teaching was not forgotten. I believed in infinite potential and still do. And with infinite potential, let's focus on the body, or body/mind.

The body can be seen as a tool we use to perceive and interact with life around us. Let's pretend the body is just an ordinary tool, such as a hammer. Can a hammer catch a cold? Of course not. It is just a physical tool. There is a misperception that "I" am the body. We are not focused on "I" as the eternal and everlasting, infinite "I". The sickness is just a case of mistaken identity. What part of us gets sick? At the point of separation from God, one knows one is now fallible, vulnerable. This creates fear. The fear perpetuates itself in the collective mind of humanity until the thoughts become concrete and manifest into illness. But we created the illness from our confusion in believing in separation from God.

Sickness is a misperception of what is really happening. If complete and vibrant health is a possibility, then there are just different levels of health, on a continuum from more well to less well. But it is still under the umbrella of wellness or health. This leaves us without the duality of sickness and health. Another example of this is the perception of darkness and light. Light is never completely absent, it's just that our eyes are limited and only perceive certain levels. This means there can be no such thing as darkness, just different levels of light.

Note: This health information is the opinion of the author and does not replace medical advice. Please consult your health professional!

EXERCISE:

Analyze the germ theory and its truth in relation to Oneness. Write about how this hypothesis has affected you.

_____
_____
_____
_____
_____
_____
_____
_____
_____
_____
_____
_____
_____
_____
_____
_____
_____
_____
_____
_____
_____
_____
_____
_____

CHAPTER 5 - THOUGHT

THOUGHT

What is the purpose of thought? A thought is not something in the here and now… it is a trip away from the present. To entertain a thought, one must spend time away from what is happening now to fantasize about a situation, scenario, person, problem, etc. Right now, only the actual experience is real. The mind loves to make commentary on the experience it is having. The thoughts are an interpretation of the experience after the fact, similar to an echo. Do you want to spend the majority of your life listening to an echo? You can choose to think any thought at any time. All thoughts exist as potential things to think about, but they only exist as our reality in the instant we choose to think them. When one believes their thoughts, they live in a fantasy – something that doesn't exist right now. We can choose to go down any number of rabbit holes or trails away from the present, but they only lead away from what is True.

But doesn't one need to think? How does one plan the day and know what to do next? One can continue to think, but start by monitoring the thoughts and see which ones are truly helpful and which ones are just chatter or fantasy. The more this is done, the less one will use the mind for meaningless thoughts, and will function more efficiently. It is similar to defragging your hard drive. The useless information will be wiped clean and reveal a more peaceful, efficient state which will lead to functioning from a higher level of Awareness. When one is Aware, one is present and alert. They are open to Grace. As Grace takes over, the need for thought will fall away on its own.

A thought is not something in the here and now… it is a trip away from the present.

Subtle Thought

Subtle thought is a thought or network of thoughts that underlie a single thought. It's the thoughts we don't even know are in there on a deeper level until they rise to the surface. For instance, if the thought occurs "it's 9 o'clock," it usually doesn't stop there. The time is interpreted in how it relates to our life and our reaction to that. "Oh, man! I'm gonna be late…this always happens…. how will I get there in time?" This might actually be thought, or might just be felt as a panic or rushing.

When one checks the time on a clock, they will make further assessments about time with the background or subtle thoughts. These are the thoughts we do not even realize we are having. They are usually based in the past, of how we experienced time before or incidents that occurred. These experiences were locked in as the way it is. Seldom do we experience just the current situation free of past baggage. Our reaction may be physiological in that the body may experience change in blood pressure, breathing, etc. all due to a reaction to a thought about the time.

These thoughts come directly from one's belief system about the object of thought. For instance, if one believes there is not enough time, when one notices the time, a network of thought and memories is triggered about lack of time. This pulls one into a place of fear and resistance to what is happening. Once the mind comments on the situation, it is no longer present with the

Reality behind the thoughts. If one is aware of this subtle dialog occurring, one can find the outdated belief and chose to change it to a more positive one.

Writing about one's thinking is helpful and helps to realize the train of thought and where it leads to. If we see all of this on paper, we realize what we really think about time. This could then turn into a whole web of thoughts about time, about what has happened before, such as being late or rushing. It could lead to emotions about time and about life, and on and on and on. The mind can take a thought and run with it. Following the train of thought back to the first instance of this pattern we can remember gives clues to the actual origin of the pattern. We can trace them to the core of the problem, and find the issues we are trying to unearth and heal. Just having conscious awareness of the issue begins the healing process.

EXERCISE:

Throughout the day today, constantly monitor your thoughts and see what you actually think about. Are they helpful and constructive, or do they wander aimlessly from topic to topic? Are your thoughts predominantly positive or negative? Do you think of others, or are you indulging in self centered thought? Are you thinking just for the fun of it? What is the purpose of your thoughts? Are you trying to solve a problem, singing a song, or gossiping? What is underneath thought? Try writing about some of it here:

_____
_____
_____
_____
_____
_____
_____
_____
_____

_____

_____

_____

_____

_____

_____

_____

_____

_____

_____

_____

MIND

The term "mind" is a man-made concept to explain and give location to the origin of thought. We are taught that there is a thing called the "mind." The notion of "mind" is used to describe where thought comes from. It is also commonly believed that thought originates in and is interpreted in a physical location, such as the brain. Where is the mind? Many think it is the actual brain or describes what is in the brain. According to Deepak Chopra's *How to Know God*, when scientists and researchers examine the brain, they find no such explanation or location of storage of thought or anything such as the "mind".

Could it be that the mind is everywhere? Anything that occurs happens in your mind. If the situation were outside and unattached to your mind, how would you perceive it? The senses allow you to experience what is going on around you, but they are integral in the experience, a part of it. They are the part of the mind labeled "vision", "hearing", etc. Let's suppose there is only the universal faculty of perception itself, and we all have that. No one has ownership rights to perceiving. The mind is just an extra way to break information down even further, even though this is rarely needed. It interprets and categorizes data. More often than not, it is a distraction to the process of Knowing, but our society values data. We are taught to think and to claim thoughts as our own early on.

It is assumed the mind is an individual possession, rather than a Universal one. Maybe all thought comes from the common field of consciousness. Picture layers of thoughts like layers of earth in the Grand Canyon, from lowest to highest. Maybe one just tunes into the different frequencies or layers of mind and finds thoughts that mirror one's level of understanding. It is just the one mind we are all tapped into, rather than individual minds. If one takes into account the foundational truth "ALL is One", this would make sense, that there is no separation or individual mind. There would only be the one. Truth is very literal. All is One means exactly that. So, when one thinks oneself to be a separate individual, only then can one claim the thoughts as one's own.

Nonetheless, thought exists and is experienced. The Mind is a wonderful tool when one is in charge of it, but not when one is the victim of it. Most people experience the mind as rambling on, cluttered, scattered, or foggy at times. It can be under or over active. Meditation is a great way to calm the chatter of the mind and develop discipline of thought, so one is the boss of the mind, and it, a tool. If it is lazy, one can strengthen it through focus, activity and stimulation, such as reading.

The mind is not separate from the body. The mind explains the body to itself. For example, when your toe hurts, you are not aware of this until the mind tells you. Then you know – OW! That hurt! But not before the mind interprets the body's experience.

When the mind is healthy, one can access thoughts or memories at will. This ability is compromised when one is limited by beliefs to the contrary. Some of these hindering beliefs might be: Memory declines with age, or I have a bad memory, or the like. These are limitations one subscribes to because they think that is the way it is, it has to be that way, and have seen others experience these things. But that is only one option. Many allow such limitations due to the fact they are unaware there is a choice. They can become resigned to these limitations because they think there is no other way. Once these thoughts are seen as part of a limiting belief system and discarded, and proper nutrition is applied, one can turn this and other similar complaints around. There are people who have learned to keep the brain active all their lives and overcome limitations. You can too.

Are you your mind? If you stop thinking…are you still there?

STRIVING

According to Webster's dictionary, the term 'striving' means "to exert much effort or energy; to struggle in opposition." Striving is motivated by a belief in lack. Depending on motive, people can strive to give or to get. Some strive to be a better person, or to be loving or helpful. Some strive for expensive cars, successful careers, more than they currently have – whatever is bigger and better. They may be looking for material gain, excitement, accomplishment or love – it doesn't matter. The fact that they are striving means they do not feel at peace or that they have what they need right now. Because they are under the impression that there is something to get, to be, or to do that will make them feel complete, they strive to get it. Other words for this are grasping, clutching, seeking, yearning, longing, pushing – you get the idea. They are struggling to find happiness and peace. But where are these found?

Most are looking for it in the material world which cannot provide the ultimate and eternal fulfillment. This world is designed to have infinite possibilities, which is wonderful, but it also has infinite distractions. One can always find another material object to covet and possess. There is always a new product advertisers tell us we "need" or a new technology available. This phenomena not only includes stuff, but also desires, thoughts, emotions, emotional fulfillment, etc.

These finite distractions are all temporary - what could be called "horizontal" as they keep going infinitely outwards in all directions. The term horizontal means spread out in every direction like the horizon, but only on a flat plane. This is far from the completeness of multi-dimensional planes. When something is horizontal, there is no vertical growth. Focusing on the material world can only yield growth in a limited or finite way.

Infinite fulfillment and happiness cannot be found in material things. The nature of the world is impermanence – that is to say the only thing that is constant is change. Nothing stays the same. Everything that is alive, dies. All things eventually wear out. This is not negative thinking, but realistic and practical. Our tastes and interests are made to be ever changing and curious. Nothing remains unchanged indefinitely, except the Source of change Itself. The lasting Peace is a natural faculty of the Self when the material world is not held onto. The world will come and go, but what we are as our infiniteness remains unchanged.

Striving is a mechanism of something that is unfulfilled. One has to first feel empty before they look for something to fill the hole. The feeling of lack of fulfillment leads us to search for True Fulfillment, or God. Emptiness is the magnet that attracts its other half. This is a good thing, in that the emptiness magnet continues to attract things until it gets filled. It is attracted to its' exact answer, or to the point in which it has no more polarity or opposite in which to attract more. So, at first if one feels unfulfilled, and wants instant gratification or thinks they will be happy with material things, they will then search for it in things they find appealing: food, sex, cars, etc. But eventually this does not satisfy and the attraction to True Fulfillment grows stronger.

The magnet further defines itself. A more permanent happiness is the goal and one can then begin to attract the tools to help one find a more lasting joy in being a loving person with higher values. This process brings a higher level of awareness, and a more positive way of life. These higher and more positive states expand and define the magnetic capacity further. So now one is aware of and looking for a permanent and lasting love – one now knows it is possible and attracts higher level tools to realize the Self. In this beautiful unfolding that Grace has designed, we see how it is inevitable that one is always led and has the opportunity to move toward Grace. It is possible the more one is uncomfortable in that perceived separation, the more one looks for Peace. Suffering is a method of salvation or return to Peace. Once one sees that one was always on the path, one can rest in the ultimate design, that "destiny can then be certain," in the words of David Hawkins (Hawkins 2002, 292.) No need for striving anymore.

EXERCISE:

Take notice of where you are striving or exerting too much effort in your daily life. How does it feel? Use this as an opportunity to ask yourself "Is what I am doing make me feel happy and fulfilled?" Take time to notice and make course corrections back to what you are seeking through your actions. Make a list of what really matters to you. Note how these positive things make you feel. Hold this feeling and remember the things that matter as you go about your day.

The things that matter most to me are: _____

_____

_____

_____

_____

_____

_____

CHAPTER 6 – LOVE, FORGIVENESS AND PEACE

LOVE

Love is a word that is often used but seldom fully felt or understood. There are many levels or experiences of love. Among them are conditional love, unconditional love, and Universal or Divine love.

Conditional love is most prevalent. It is often performance based. Love is granted or there when the conditions are right. Example: If we are good, we achieve, we appease. There are often expectations and strings attached. Another perception is that it is felt "from" or someone, in words or actions. When one feels loving or loved, this feeling is a limited perception of love. If we look at why we love, the reason is often for our own self, not to benefit the other. We often love someone because we think we may get something from them – happiness, security, companionship, etc. It is a fickle love and doesn't provide stability and the reassurance of trust and commitment.

Unconditional Love is beyond what most know as the typical human experience of love. It loves for love's sake and seeks to give and build others. Regardless of circumstances, the love remains the same. This is distinct from Divine love, in that we still only love certain people this much and not all are equal from this standpoint. We are still playing favorites and the Divine doesn't discriminate.

Divine Love is beyond the dualistic idea of love, where there is something or someone else to love. One is Love Itself. If ALL is love, why would love not radiate from everything? Universal Love is all inclusive. It includes all races, all species, all beings, period. All are held in reverence. All glistens and is profound. All is one thing – Love manifest. Being in awe of creation and having respect for each aspect allows for the experience of Universal Love.

DEVOTION

From love we can experience and develop devotion. Devotion is an honoring of that which we love. It is giving over to that love, taking action for and deriving one's purpose from that. It brings one joy to share this love. It appears that doing so is life's new purpose. The enthusiasm and momentum of love allows one to act with devotion towards all of life - to devote oneself to the task of recognizing, serving and furthering this love for all time.

FORGIVENESS

Unconditional and Divine love also allow for complete healing in relationships in the form of forgiveness. Whatever happened in the past, whether 5 minutes, 5 days or 5 years ago, is released. When we hold grudges, we hold onto our ideas of how it should have been, or our idea of the right way. Our lack of acceptance of people as they are, stamps a big "rejection" on their forehead saying they "should" be different than they are. Forgiveness does not mean one is a doormat and allows wrongful or abusive behavior. One can still point out proper rules of fair play while in a space of non-judgment and forgiveness. Sometimes things need to be discussed or processed before they are released. This assures a complete letting go so one doesn't unknowingly carry negative energy with them. Forgiveness releases ourselves as much as anyone. Allow yourself to be free of finding fault. Focus on solutions. And Peace.

PEACE

Is it common to hear people speak of and ask for peace – world peace, may those that have died rest in peace, etc. People say that they would like "peace and quiet." Why do all want peace? Peace is an aspect of our true nature. It is natural to want that, although most have never experienced true peace. True peace comes from recognizing the stillness and unlimited nature of our being always present. It is open and free, unburdened. Initially it is easier to notice in stillness. Once it is experienced, it is more easily felt again, because there is a reference point for Peace. The trick then, is to find it in the world that is seemingly chaotic and choose to see the peace that is inherent in all things. It is always there to be tuned into and honored.

PEACE

The solid Rock
That faithfully supports
Precious life
Goes unnoticed, yet is ALL.
Contained within every droplet of Life,
There is radiance and Light
Tranquility and stillness
Silence and awe of Existence.
Release, surrender into That.
The fulfilling freedom
Of the pervasive Void brings rest,
Opens and allows gratitude
Cleanses and makes the world new.
May Eternal Peace fill you.

Chapter 7 – Reality and Identity

What is Real?

Now it is being determined that objects in the physical reality are less solid matter than originally thought. They are comprised mostly of space. In fact, it seems even the "solid" atomic molecules are not even solid, but mostly space. What holds everything together? Our thoughts have a big role in the way things appear. If you've seen the movie on quantum physics "What The Bleep Do We Know?" you know what I'm talking about. We have labeled molecules and all their parts, labeling the roles they play and how everything works. This is our interpretation of the world around us. We decipher things and according to our assessment, call them facts. These theories are based on partial evidence as we do not and cannot know all of the variables in any given situation. It is always an assumption or hypothesis. Reality always depends on context.

Here is an example of what I mean: originally, someone devised the system of mathematics. In the basic mathematical system, 2+2=4, right? Yes, but only as a mathematical equation. This only works in this one limited system. What if I take it out of this context and make up a new system….I assign a different value to the number 2, such as 2=sadness. With this equation,

2+2 might not equal 4. So, the system of mathematics is valuable and we agree to use it as a way of communicating in the world. But it does not mean it is the most effective, or the only way to communicate. We can only see such a small piece of the big picture. Our current systems are only one way to look at information, leaving many choices we could use to understand the world. Up to this point, we have collectively agreed upon a basic model by which to function. We have then made an assumption based on our model that "this is how the world works." If you do not use this system, then what you believe or see is not widely accepted as valid and true.

Another broader viewpoint might be that there are infinite possibilities - that our limited reality is subjective because it is viewed through the senses. This means individual interpretation through the senses varies from person to person and therefore everything is open to subjective interpretation. In this scenario, the experiencer and the object are not separate. The object cannot be assessed without considering the subjective person viewing it. They are not separate, but interacting and affecting each other. So what do we actually perceive? The One interacting with itself.

SUBJECTIVE REALITY

The only reality that can be known is that which one perceives through the personal senses…sight, sound, touch, smell, taste, knowing or intuition. Once we perceive something, where are the senses interpreted? When something has been seen, it is not interpreted in the eye. The information goes from the eye to the brain and then the mind says "I see it." The mind interprets the information: I smell something….I hear something…..etc. These are all faculties of the mind. All of the senses are one tool - the tool of perception. We use the senses to access and experience the mind. This is the only way we can know the world – through our subjective perception. Even what we perceive as external objective Truth comes through a subjective filter into one's awareness. We can no longer falsely interpret our surroundings as external. Everything is Within. Anything that is perceived as outside of ourselves is only a projection.

If reality is subjective, why would we need others to validate anything about ourselves? We look to others for approval or disapproval. Are we loved, are we right, are we safe, are we OK? Only we know the answer. Others cannot validate our world, because they only have a concept of what it should be from the outside looking in. They can only validate our experience from their experience of it. They can know our experience from what we tell them or they observe – what we seem to be doing, seeing, thinking, etc. Even if we trust another, the decision to do so was based on information gathered through the senses. The senses can be cleared of obstructions and honed for accuracy and to have right discrimination. One way to do this is with spiritual practices and purification. Then our interpretation can be clear and positive.

When we trust our own interpretation, we see that our senses are the direct link to our relationship with the world. No other validation needed or even possible. We live in "Self Infinity"- a state of autonomy in which one is free from the bondage of illusion or false understanding. Self Infinity is when we take complete responsibility for ourselves, our lives, our reactions and perceptions. When there is no other, there is no one to blame, no victim or perpetrator. We are free from the world of projection and live in the world peacefully without attachment or aversion.

Our senses are our direct relationship to the world, no other validation needed.
We live in "Self Infinity".

Jennifer D. Ables, PhD

How do we measure our worth?

Worth may not be something we think of consciously, but from childhood on up, we are comparing and contrasting ourselves with others. We want to know how we measure up, where we rank. How we feel about ourselves may depend on what others have said in the past or how they reacted to us as a person. What was reflected back to us? Are we important, are we loved? Are we interesting? If we do not receive validation in ways that confirm our worth, wounds may form. These wounds can grow deeper over time and be reinforced in future interactions as the truth, emerging again and again as patterns in our lives. From a conscious standpoint, we can heal these patterns through introspection and inner child work. We can look to the Truth that we are perfect and whole. Doing so can heal the old misperception. Then there is the potential for internal validation instead of looking to others for confirmation of our worth. What do we know for certain about ourselves? How do you picture yourself as an adult? Ask - Am I worth having enough rest, a happy experience, someone's respect?

You are here for others to experience the *real* you, whatever that is. Your worth is automatic when you are you. It is a given. You are priceless. And you deserve all things wonderful that life has to offer. A common feeling is: "I shouldn't have wonderful things when there are people who have less." When we affirm our worth, it helps others accept more for themselves and become aware of their worth. It is not a divine or noble thought to suffer because others are suffering. This type of thinking does not help them and does not help you. As we allow happiness and prosperity in our lives, we set an example for others. First of all, happiness definitely rubs off. Enthusiasm, like laughter, is absolutely contagious. This will help all who come in contact with it. Second, it gives others a sense that happiness is possible and permission to experience it.

Another thing we use to assess our value is our identity – who we are. We have roles we play in the world, and traits we possess that we define ourselves by. We also have expectations of how we should fulfill these. By scrutinizing ourselves in these roles, we make a value judgment. For instance, a person may believe appearance is part of his/her value. If the person does not like his/her appearance, the person will think of him/herself as being lower in value. If the person thinks he/she looks great, he/she will feel a sense of worth. Value is not something we look like, or do. It is inherent in who we are. We are valuable because we exist. The specialness is not from anything in particular. Just loving others and letting them experience us as we are is the gift, or has value. Nothing can have much more value than that. Your intent and sincerity to be real with others will be all that is needed.

EXERCISE:

List the things about you that are used to determine your worth. See how they are superficial and secondary to who you really are? Tell yourself you are priceless and important because you exist. Example:

Determining factor	Reason or Scenario	Truth
1. Money	I don't have much money, therefore I am not important	Money does not determine my worth
2.		
3.		
4.		
5.		
6.		

"I am priceless and important because I exist."

LEARNING WHO YOU'RE NOT

We are infiniteness, everything in its fullness. If we are everything, there is nothing to define. Then the process of coming to know ourselves as infiniteness becomes more and more abstract, more non-descript. It is hard to learn what one is, but the one thing we can learn about is who or what we are not. We do this by examining our use of labels. We use labels to define things, to communicate to each other. Labels by nature separate one thing from another. Anything we can label stands apart and becomes distinct from what is not that. For our identity, labels instill a sense of individuality or a separate sense of I. When we remove the labels from ourselves and others, we recognize the sense of universality or sameness underneath.

EXERCISE:

Who do you think you are? Make a list of everything you think you are or associate as you/yours. This includes preferences, physical and personality traits, titles/roles and all descriptive adjectives (nice and not so nice.) An example might be "my favorite color is blue" or "I love hamsters." These labels keep you from enjoying the rest of the colors and animals as much as the favored ones. As you release the focus on these, you find you are not only that. Remember, you are not losing anything. You are simply taking your attention off the label and putting it back on everything - all the labels - and loving everything the same. The great thing about learning who you're not is that this points to who you really are.

_____

_____

_____

_____

_____

_____

_____
_____
_____
_____
_____
_____
_____
_____
_____
_____
_____
_____
_____
_____
_____
_____
_____
_____
_____
_____
_____

CHAPTER 8 – SELF AWARENESS AND THE ENERGETIC SYSTEM

THE ENERGETIC SYSTEM

Whether we are aware of it or not, each one of us has an energetic system. This system is part of the collective energetic system of all life and the world around us. The physical body has an energetic structure that permeates and surrounds it. These energetic bodies, as they are called, are made up of vital or life force energy. Sometimes called the subtle system because it exists on a more subtle or energetic level and is not considered visible to the naked eye. Just like a computer, it contains information and programming. The information stored in the energetic layers is the contents of the being - the person's emotions, mental/psychological, and spiritual information. It also contains an energetic blueprint of the physical body. The energetic system is a book of who we are - past, present and future. This system is a dynamic aspect of our being, allowing us to know and interpret our lives from an energetic vantage point. By assessment and interaction with the energetic bodies, we can learn about ourselves and heal deeper issues. Clearing and healing this system can help one spiritually raise in awareness by clearing out old perceptions and having more clarity. Qualities can be assessed, balanced and enhanced. There are many ways to work with the energetic system. Usually, a developed sensitivity or intuition helps us tune into the subtle system and its contents.

WHAT IS INTUITION?

Intuition is inner guidance, sensitivity and deepening of the senses that allows a fuller interpretation of the world. It is a useful tool to further positive experience and personal growth. We use intuition to strengthen and confirm our perception and to gain information about our reality. Intuition may come in different ways: through sight, sound, knowingness, feeling or other impressions or interpretations. As intuition develops, one becomes more confident and the information is trusted and understood.

There are many different ways to access one's intuition. In the physical world, we use our senses to navigate. On an energetic or subtle level, one can use intuition to hear, picture or see, know or feel what's True. If this does not come completely naturally to you, don't worry. You can learn more about how to connect in this way, and with practice, you will develop it. The more one practices, intuition becomes a part of one's being and happens naturally and spontaneously. Sometimes a skill comes naturally or develops over time, and sometimes it is not one of the main faculties through which one automatically functions. One faculty (i.e. visual, auditory or other means of gathering information about the world) is usually stronger than others. Let's look at intuition in this perspective and how it can be applied using different techniques. The emphasis is on encouraging the development of one's own true Knowing.

Self Awareness

How well do you know your True Self? Self awareness is a significant part of our evolution and growth. By studying who and what we are, we discover more about our potential. This discovery allows us to be more of who we are and manifest our potential as more loving, peaceful and effective beings.

Intuition is a tool we can use to know ourselves better and have awareness of our true nature. Intuition or inner guidance is an accurate way of getting information. As we open and clear our subtle system, we become like an open window for the Divine energy that flows through us. This brings a higher awareness and perception. We are capable of more balance, insight and better overall health when we are clear.

It is also quite beneficial to gain higher body awareness. Some people are not aware of what or how they are feeling, whether they have pain or not, and others know the exact location of the problem or in what organ it originates. The more we know about ourselves, the more we can consciously heal.

How well do you know your True Self?

Visualization

When someone suggests that you "picture" something or "see it in the mind's eye," to what are they referring? They are referring to an ability we have to see beyond seeing with our physical eyes. It is a way of interpreting information in a visual format in the brain that helps us connect with the world around us and ourselves.

When one is using the perceptual tool of clairvoyance or intuitive sight, one is seeing beyond the physical into more subtle levels or dimensions. One way to help yourself learn to do this is to "imagine" what might be there. Just "go there" in your mind and see what you find. This doesn't sound very scientific, but it is surprisingly accurate. We'll let science fill in the details about how it works in a few years.

Another way is to practice seeing the energy or aura of plants, animals and people. Look at the light or energy around different people and compare. Look at people's energy - what colors do you see? What does it convey visually? Learn to interpret what you see by recording your information. Pick one thing and record how it changes over time. You will learn what specific colors or phenomena mean for you as a general rule.

Many times what you see visually will correspond with what you see energetically. For instance, if someone's body has large shoulders, one might see that the energy in that area seems stronger or maybe blocked or stuck in that part of the body. Another example might be someone who has very small, skinny legs. Usually the aura or energy around the legs appears depleted or not very bright. They may appear less heavy or to not be very connected to the ground.

EXERCISE:

Check your own energy. Try assessing your energy at different times of the day, like when you are fresh in the morning, or tired later in the day. How does it appear different? How does is change with your attention? Through investigation, you will teach yourself about intuitive sight. Write about what you find: _____

_____
_____
_____
_____
_____
_____
_____
_____

CHAPTER 9 - SURRENDER

PRAYER OF SURRENDER AND DEDICATION

Creator/Source/Divine Presence, I ask to be of the utmost service. Allow me to surrender to the bigger picture so I can serve in the highest capacity, to be Love to those close to me and the extended circle of lives I touch. I ask for clarity and focus. I ask to be aware of and guided as to Priority at all times. I pray to be an example of ease and balance and to be an expression of Universal Love. I pray to be Joy of Life manifest. I pray for strength of character, courage and follow through. I now rededicate my life and entire being for service as a higher expression of Truth - to be a manifestation of Compassion and Freedom for others. I pray for guidance and validation as to the capacity and gifts in which I have to share. I ask for the ability to Trust all is provided. I pray for further direction and resources to more effectively serve. I surrender any and all agendas in order for the highest good to manifest. I now relinquish all so Divine Will is fully manifest through this being. I am grateful for all opportunities Grace allows.

Where Rivers Flow

Where do all rivers flow?
It is said, "to the Sea."
The River of Joy
Flows into the Sea of Grace
As does the River of Love
And the River of Peace.
There they are indistinct
From one another
As if they never existed apart.
If one bathes in the sea,
Peace may be felt,
Love may be felt,
Joy may be felt,
But these cannot be separated
From the Water.
May you bathe in the Sea of Grace eternally.

WHAT ARE YOU GOING TO DO ABOUT IT?

After reading all these words, thoughts and suggestions that are written, you might put the book down and never think about it again. Is this what you want? How are you going to use what you found out about yourself and what Is? How are you going to incorporate what you feel deeply about into your life? If anything has inspired you, what are you inspired to do? Are you going to better your community, be love to your family, study spiritual Truth? How does what you have read matter in your life and shape who you are? This is a call to action. This is where the rubber meets the road, where opportunity begins. Now is your chance. Do it.

EXERCISE:
List at least 5 actions you will take in response to what you are passionate about.

1. _____

_____

_____

2. _____

_____

_____

3. _____

_____

_____

4. _____

_____

_____

5. _____

_____

_____

GLOSSARY

Acceptance - Acceptance is allowing and fully loving a situation or issue. Not rejecting any aspect of self or life.

Devotion – An honoring of and serving that which we love. It is giving over to that love, taking action for and deriving one's purpose from that.

Duality - meaning opposites like night and day, dark and light, empty and full, etc. Duality already assumes there is a positive and a negative.

Enlightenment – a term used to describe a broad range of higher experiences and states; Spiritual Enlightenment is wisdom, clarity and understanding of what you are and what God is.

Foundational Truth – Truth found as a theme in most major religions and philosophies over time that can serve as a foundation for personal growth.

Grace – the allowance of circumstances by God. The amazing manifestation of the Divine.

Higher Self – The eternal and universal soul or consciousness that we are a part of. The non-physical or True Self.

Introspection – used interchangeably with Self inquiry, introspection means examination of one's own thoughts and feelings.

Intuition - Inner guidance, sensitivity and deepening of the senses that allows a fuller interpretation of the world. Intuition is a useful tool to further positive experience and personal growth.

Karma – The concept that action is responsible for the cycle of cause and effect. Karma can be positive or negative and is created by thoughts, words and actions.

Knowing/Knowledge – with capitol "K" refers to knowing in the sense of True spiritual wisdom.

Law of Attraction – A universal law stating that we create and attract the things in our lives.

Liberation – Complete and total Freedom from suffering and the illusions that bind humankind.

Meditation – a technique used to focus and still the mind.

mind - a man-made concept to explain and give location to the origin of thought.

Personal power - This refers to how powerful an individual feels and acts.

Release - Release is a way of getting rid of old issues or clearing blocks from your awareness.

Resistance - anything that blocks the complete Knowledge and Love of God.

Self – capitol "S" distinguishes the awakened Self, while lowercase "s" denotes egoic self.

Self Infinity – a state of autonomy in which one is free from the bondage of illusion or false understanding.

Self inquiry - the digging into your own consciousness to answer your unanswered questions.

Self Realization - A deep and lived understanding of what you are and what God is. The term is used to describe the clarity and realization of the Self.

Source – God, the origin from which all comes.

Surrender – To give oneself fully to the Divine. Surrender is what happens inside when one sees the pointlessness in the struggle and stops struggling.

Transcend - To pass beyond the old to something new.

True Self – True Self is all of Ourselves. It is pure potential of whatever we imagine it to be.

Trust – reliance on a person or thing.

Unity – A concept denoting the harmony and Oneness of all of life.

Universal – relating to the entire world or universe; the big picture.

Resources

Adyashanti. www.adyashanti.org

Amma. http://www.ammachi.org

Connor, Patrick. www.theeternalself.com

Katie, Byron. www.thework.com

Nager, Brian. www.revealingtruthnow.com

Purna, Dr Svami. http://www.adhyatmikfoundation.org

Tolle, Eckhart. http://www.eckharttolle.com

What the Bleep do We Know!? William Arntz, Betsy Chasse, Mark Vicente. Lord of the Wind Films, LLC. 2004.

References

Chopra, Deepak. *How to Know God*. Directed by Victor Frank. Los Angeles, CA: 20th Century Fox. 2006.

Hawkins, David. *Power vs. Force*. Carlsbad, California: Hay House, Inc. 2002.

Laughter, Humor and Pain Perception in Children: A Pilot Study. **Margaret Stuber, Sherry Dunay Hilber, Lisa Libman Mintzer, Marleen Castaneda, Dorie Glover and Lonnie Zeltzer.** Semel Institute at UCLA, 760 Westwood Plaza, Los Angeles, CA 90024-1759.